THE ALLEY OF SECRETS

EMERALD CITY DRAGONS - PROLOGUE

WES GRANDMONT III

WESLEYGRANDMONT.COM

The Alley of Secrets (Emerald City Dragons - Prologue) / Wes Grandmont
III.
Published by Steamfire Studios
(an imprint of Wesley Grandmont III)
www.wesleygrandmont.com

First Edition 2018 v1.0.2
ASIN: B07CKGRSTZ
ISBN: 1-7320844-0-8
ISBN-13: 978-1-73208-440-7

To my family and friends,
This story is for you.

1

KNIVES AND BODIES

The body looked like it had died from a long fall. The victim was female this time. Detective Carter Malloy lifted the yellow tape barrier surrounding the rooftop crime scene. Forensics was finishing up. Little numbered plastic tents had been placed around the area. He was careful not to disturb their work as he approached.

The overcast sky shrouded the Seattle skyline in mist. The building was the tallest within a few blocks. Its bigger neighbors were dark silhouettes in the fog. No way she could have fallen from one of them and landed up here. Carter turned toward the forensic team. "Find anything out of the ordinary?"

One of the new guys answered him—Tommy might have been his name. "Same as the others. No ID. No fingerprint match in the database. Nothing on facial recognition. Look under the coat—might remind you of something."

This was the third falling victim in as many days. None of them looked like suicides. Carter pulled on a pair of rubber surgical gloves. "Thanks, Tommy."

"It's James, sir."

Whatever, kid.

Jane Doe's arms and legs were bent at all the wrong angles. The blood had dried where it had splattered from the impact of the fall. The puddle was still wet around the body.

Carter pulled out a pen and flipped aside the blood-soaked jacket. Under her left arm was a large sheathed knife. His lips pressed together. He pulled the weapon out and dropped it into a clear plastic evidence bag. The handle was wrapped in red leather. The shiny blade had ornate symbols carved into the surface. It looked old—like an ancient ceremonial dagger. It looked like the ones he'd removed from the two John Does they'd found earlier in the week. Were these ritualistic killings? A cult or some weird serial killer? Why did every victim have the same weapon? Better yet, why hadn't they used it to defend themselves?

The woman's black leather jacket was ripped along the shoulders. Something had torn through the material and left multiple puncture wounds along her collar bones. Three deep holes on either side. Carter raised an eyebrow and looked up at the new guy. "She's got the same injuries we saw on the other two."

James nodded. "We haven't been able to identify the cause. Almost looks like they were all skewered by meat hooks."

Thanks for the imagery kid. Drops of water dotted the plastic evidence bag. It was starting to rain. Carter stood. "Any witnesses?"

"None. Maintenance found the body a few hours ago."

By the amount of dried blood, Jane Doe had taken her long fall sometime well before sunrise. The other two falling victims had been found in back alleys—pushed or thrown from one of the nearby buildings—but this woman had to have fallen from the sky. Carter pulled out his phone and made a note to check on recent flight plans whose routes might have crossed the area. One of them might provide a lead.

Carter turned the plastic wrapped blade over in his hand. He had a contact in the Anthropology department at the University that might be able to help identify the markings. "I need you to catalog this knife. I'm taking it with me."

"Sir, we were instructed to collect all—"

"Relax kid. We've got two like it in the evidence locker. I'm going to show this one to a specialist, then it'll go right into lock-up with its buddies." This James kid was starting to get annoying.

"But, we have orders—"

"I know, Jimmy. And it's going to be okay. Take the damn pictures." James's face turned red, but he was smart enough to keep his mouth shut.

One of the other forensic guys came over—an old-timer. His name was—Ken. "It's fine James. Detective Malloy has done this before. He'll have it in the locker before the end of the day. Right, Detective?"

"Have I ever let you down, Ken?"

Ken didn't answer. He pursed his lips and shook his head. Carter was almost sure he had the guy's name right. Ken took the bag, scrawled some information on the plastic with a black marker, snapped some photos, then sealed the bag with evidence tape. He handed it back to Carter. "Sign it out from the inventory list before you leave."

"Thanks, Ken."

"It's Kevin."

Damn. Wrong again.

Carter took the bag and stepped back under the yellow barrier. His memory was going to hell—seemed to be getting worse the last few years. He'd had a few blackouts. Lost a few hours one time. A whole day the other. It had freaked him out a bit, but he hadn't shared that with anyone. You start talking about stuff like that at the office and the next thing you know they're throwing you a retirement party. He tossed his gloves in one of the medical waste bags. Another forensic guy held up a pen and clipboard that listed the evidence they'd cataloged. Carter scrawled his name next to the line that said "Knife" and handed the pen back.

On the way down the elevator, he dialed Hal Grayson. Hal was his contact at the University. The man picked up on the second ring. "This is Professor Grayson."

"Hal, it's Detective Malloy with the Seattle Police Department. You helped us out a year ago."

"Carter, right? What can I do for you?"

Carter examined the plastic wrapped blade. "I've got an old knife—part of an investigation. I was hoping I could get your thoughts on it?"

"How old?"

"No idea. It's got some markings that don't look like anything I've seen before."

"Sounds interesting. There's a cafe on campus in the building next door to my office. I'll meet you there in a half hour."

"Thanks, Hal." Carter hung up. The digital numbers on the elevator ticked by as it descended. Out of the corner of his eye, he saw a flash of green light. He looked down at the knife. Did the blade glow green? Or had he imagined that?

The elevator reached the lobby. Carter shoved the plastic wrapped knife under his coat. People tended to freak out seeing weapons in public.

Hopefully, Hal had some ideas. He needed a good lead.

The car ride from downtown to the university took about twenty minutes. People always drove slow around the police cruiser. The rain didn't help either. Carter parked in one of the campus lots and strolled along a tree-lined walkway to the cafe. The late September chill was turning the leaves yellow. Water dripped from them onto the sidewalk. It had been a strange week. Three unidentified bodies—all dead from falling. Three identical knives. What was the connection?

The building that housed the cafe was ahead on the left. A modern four-story structure that looked like a random stack of brick, glass and steel cubes. Carter pushed his way through the glass doors. The cafe took up most of the lobby. Overcast light spilled in through two-story high, rain-spattered windows. The smell of fresh coffee filled the air. Sometimes Carter wished he had picked a different line of work. One that let him spend more time in happier places instead of hanging out with dead bodies.

The professor was sitting at one of the small square tables spread around the room, a thin man with graying hair and a trimmed white beard. He stood when he saw Carter approaching.

The detective held out his hand. A year ago, they both had a lot less gray. "Thanks for meeting me."

Hal shook his hand and grinned. "Not a problem. I'm a sucker for mysterious artifacts."

They sat down. Carter pulled the evidence bag out and pushed it across the table. "What do you think?"

Hal turned the plastic over pulling it tight against the blade to see the symbols. He chewed on his lip. His brows furrowed. Whatever Hal was going to tell him was not good news. Carter scanned the faces of the people at the nearby tables while he waited.

The professor set the bag down and sat back in his chair. "It's not an ancient language I've seen. To be honest, I don't think this is a real artifact."

"What is it then?"

Hal gestured out the windows. "There's a campus club here for students that are interested in cosplay."

"Cosplay?"

"Dressing up like fictional characters from games, movies, and comics to attend conventions."

"What does that have to do—"

"I think this knife is a prop. These markings are something invented by an artist. It's not a real language."

"So, you think someone made this for fun? It seems too well crafted for a prop."

"A lot of conventions and renaissance fairs come through the area. I'd suggest looking at some of the specialty sword and knife vendors. They sell these sorts of fantasy blades."

Carter pulled the plastic bag back across the table. It wasn't what he'd been expecting, but it was a lead—more than he'd had an hour ago. "Let's say you're right. Any idea what game, movie or comic this thing is based on?"

"I'm not into that sort of thing. You could try a comic shop. The clerks are knowledgeable."

"Fair enough. Thanks for your time, Hal." Carter pulled out his wallet and slid a five-dollar bill and his card across the table. "Next latte is on me. If you think of anything else, call me."

They shook hands. Carter exited into the cold autumn air. While he walked to the car, he took another look at the blade. Just a prop? What would three unidentifiable dead people be doing with three fantasy knives? Maybe if he could find the manufacturer, he could track down where the blades had been sold. Forensics had an image recognition system designed to scrape the web for matches to crime scene photos. It might be able to find a site selling them.

Carter passed a student while he was examining the blade. She gave him a weird look. He stuffed the evidence bag back under his jacket. No need to freak the kids out. Halloween wasn't for another month.

———————

It was four o'clock by the time he arrived at the Precinct. He'd promised to have the knife back in the evidence locker by the end of the day. The sooner, the better. It was awkward to carry—he should have brought a briefcase to put it in. The officer on duty at the locker was named Mary. He was certain this time because it said *Mary* on the name tag above her shirt pocket.

"Hi, Mary. I've got a piece of evidence to check in. Promised I'd have it back by the end of the day." He withdrew the plastic bag from his jacket and set it on the counter.

Mary typed something into her computer. "Looks like you missed the courier."

"What courier?"

"A court order came in an hour or so ago to have the knives returned to their owner."

"Someone took evidence from my open investigations?"

Mary shook her head. "I know, seemed strange to me too. The Chief authorized it."

"Seriously?" He took the bag off the counter. "Well, I'm not losing this one."

"You know you can't take that home."

Carter felt his face getting hot. "Yeah, I'm aware. I'm going to get some answers. I'll bring it back soon." He headed toward the elevator. Why would his boss sabotage an open case?

The Chief of Police's office was on the fourth floor. Kathleen O'Brien preferred scheduled meetings. Carter opened the door to her office without knocking. He held up the plastic bag. "How am I supposed to do my job, when you're giving away my evidence, Kathy?"

"Good afternoon, Carter. Please come in." Her gaze stabbed through him. He was overstepping—he didn't care.

Carter set the blade down on her desk. "Why would you let someone take evidence from an open investigation?"

"Sit down. Now."

He pushed aside one of the chairs in front of her desk and sat.

"When the court issues an order, I don't get the luxury of ignoring it. Neither do you."

Carter pulled out a stick of gum and began to chew. Kathy hated the sound of people smacking on food. "Who has the pull to get a court order like that?"

The Chief glared at him. "I'm glad you asked." She slid a black business card across the desk.

Carter leaned forward and picked it up. *Rakman & Associates* was printed in silver foil across the front. "Who the hell are these guys? A law firm?"

"I'm not sure. You can ask them yourself."

Carter stopped chewing. "What do you mean?"

The Chief smiled—not in a nice way. "I mean you're

going to go there right now and deliver this knife to them, then come straight back here so I know it's done."

"I'm not—"

"Shut up, Carter. You'll do it. And you'll do it before their offices close in an hour. You'll do it because if you don't, you'll be patrolling for parking violations for the next six months."

Carter pulled the bag off her desk and stood. He knew when a battle was lost. His mistake was coming in angry. He should have taken a moment to calm down. Stupid. Now he was going to have to play errand boy and cripple his investigation. He opened the door to leave.

"Oh, and Carter—"

He turned.

"Next time, knock."

He nodded and forced a smile on his face. As he headed toward the elevator, Carter looked at the card again. The address for the firm was in the Columbia Center Tower. Why would these guys need a matching collection of fantasy knives? Had the victims all been employees?

He stopped at his desk and grabbed the crime scene photos of the victim's faces. Maybe someone at *Rakman & Associates* would recognize one of them—or maybe they'd pretend they didn't. Either way, he might have another lead. Carter stuffed the photos and the blade into a briefcase and headed towards the lobby.

RAKMAN & ASSOCIATES

Anyone who had enough influence to remove evidence from an open investigation, was someone who knew enough about the situation to decide it was worth exercising that power. Carter was going to get answers, but he'd have to be careful. He was supposed to be returning property—not chatting them up.

The Columbia Center Tower's windows reflected the surrounding buildings. It was enormous, the tallest building West of the Mississippi, rising nearly a thousand feet into the sky. The business card said *Rakman & Associates* was in Suite 7117. Carter entered the lobby's atrium carrying his briefcase. His wet shoes squeaked on the polished granite floors as he made his way to a bank of elevators. He punched the up button and waited. The investigation could go on without the knives. He had the forensic photos and no reason to believe they were involved in the deaths of the three victims. It was the principle of it that irritated him.

The elevator arrived. Two people in dark clothing, a man, and a woman got in with him. Carter tapped the button for floor 71. The pair didn't hit any buttons. They rode up in silence. Carter glanced at them in the polished metal of the door. Over the years he'd gotten good at telling whether a person had seen combat. They had a way of watching their surroundings without appearing like they were watching—like these two were doing right now. He studied his own reflection to take his mind off them. Years ago, he had a full scalp of brown hair. Now the gray in his sideburns was creeping up his head like a winter frost. His hairline was receding and he needed a shave. At least he hadn't put on too much weight. Carter's ears popped as the elevator slowed and the doors opened onto the 71st floor. He waited for his two friends to get off before he followed.

The lobby was decorated in dark tones. The floor was polished black granite. The walls were covered in dark paneled wood. A fountain behind the desk trickled down a slab of slate into a trough filled with smooth black stones. Recessed lighting in the ceiling provided some warmth. The only bright colors were the pale marble top of the reception desk and a silver vase filled with lilies sitting on a white table in the center of the lobby.

The two strangers entered a door to the right of the desk. Carter wasn't certain he was in the correct place. There was no sign or plaque indicating that this was *Rakman & Associates*. He walked around the flowers and approached the desk.

A woman in a dark suit sat behind it. She looked up as he drew near. "May I help you?"

"I'm here to see Rakman." He wasn't, but since he didn't have another name it was worth a shot.

"Do you have an appointment?"

"My name is Detective Malloy. I'm with the Seattle Police Department. I'm returning some property to him."

"Just a moment." She picked up a telephone, exchanged

some quiet words and then hung up. "He'll see you now. Through the door to the left there."

A section of the wood paneled wall swung inward revealing a hidden doorway.

"Fancy." He adjusted his grip on the briefcase and headed through the door.

Carter was in a long dark hallway that ended in a polished steel door. As he walked down the corridor, the metal door slid open. He stepped through and was standing in an enormous office. It was at least twenty yards wide and was mostly empty. Stuffed leather chairs faced a wide desk made of black wood. Behind it stood a man whose back was to Carter. He must have been looking at the view. The entire back wall of the office was a floor to ceiling plate-glass window and offered a stunning view of the city.

"Detective Malloy. So nice of you to drop by." The man didn't turn around.

Carter walked across the room. His footsteps echoing in the open space. "Rakman?"

"Leopold Rakman." The man turned. He was thin— almost skeletal. He wore a black pin-striped suit with a purple tie. A pair of wire rimmed glasses perched on the end of his sharp nose. "Please have a seat, Detective." He gestured to one of the chairs.

Carter sat in the closest one. The padded leather chair looked and felt expensive.

"I understand you have some property you'd like to return to me?"

Carter smiled. "One of your knives. I've been investigating some unusual deaths the last few days. Every victim has had one."

"Ah, yes. I became aware of this only recently myself. It is quite unfortunate. The knives are part of a private collection. Very valuable. I appreciate you returning them."

Carter opened his briefcase. He took out the forensic photos and tossed them onto the desk. "Recognize any of these people?"

Rakman collected the scattered photos and lined them up on his desk. "Yes, I'm afraid I do know them. I know them all." He looked up.

Carter's eyebrow twitched. "Who are they?"

"That information is classified, Detective."

Carter's jaw clenched. He was wading into dangerous territory, but Rakman's answers could help close the investigations. "I have three dead bodies that you've positively identified. People you know. I can't just ignore that."

"Have you ever seen the CIA Memorial Wall in Langley, Detective?"

"Only pictures."

"There's a star on that wall for every Agent who sacrificed their life in service to this country. Some with no names."

"Are you saying the victims were undercover CIA operatives?"

"They served a role just as vital to the security of this nation. It's imperative their identities remain classified."

"So, you're a federal organization?"

"If you have more questions, I suggest you take them up with your Chief and Judge Smithson. May I have the knife?"

Rakman was apparently done being cooperative. Carter opened the briefcase and set the blade on the desk. "One more thing, Mr. Rakman. All your people died from falls. All of them had puncture marks along their collar bones. Any idea what happened?"

Rakman's face tightened. "I have my suspicions."

"Should I be expecting to see more of your people showing up dead around town?"

"I sincerely hope not, Detective."

Fantastic. "I'm going to quote you as having confirmed the identity of the victims in my case file."

Rakman pushed his spectacles up his nose with a slender pinky. "Your files will most likely be redacted once they are in the system."

Carter shook his head and tried not to laugh. "Thanks for your time." Normally, this would be when he offered his card but there was no point. He closed his briefcase and stood.

Leopold Rakman gestured towards the door. "Thank you for returning the knife, Detective. The hallway leads back to the elevator. Have a pleasant evening."

The view of the city behind the desk was impressive. The lights in the surrounding buildings made them look like giant pieces of crystal. Carter enjoyed it for a moment—partly because it was beautiful—partly because it was satisfying to let Leo bask in the awkward silence.

Rakman tapped his thumb on the desk. "Detective can I—"

Carter turned and stalked towards the hallway, letting whatever else the old man had to say hang in the air. It was petty, but he didn't like getting pushed around. The door slid closed behind him and opened at the far end of the hallway. He exited into the dark lobby and crossed to the elevator.

There was a woman waiting. She had the look of the two strangers he'd ridden up with—a soldier. She glanced at him—or rather she appeared to do a threat assessment. He smiled and she turned back around. She had short blond hair and a tailored green leather riding jacket. Carter wondered if she had one of the strange blades hidden underneath it.

The elevator arrived and they both got on. Carter had an idea. It was a bad idea. It was obvious this case was meant to be closed without a proper resolution, but that wasn't why he'd gotten into this line of work. He wasn't even close to a dead-end yet. There were too many unanswered questions —and not just about the victims. *Rakman & Associates* was a front for something—but what? How did they have so much influence? What were they doing in the city that had to remain so secret? If he followed this woman, maybe he could get information that would help answer some of his questions.

The elevator stopped at the lobby and the doors opened. The woman took out a phone and walked towards one of the exits. Carter followed at a slower pace, allowing the gap between them to grow. He wished he wasn't carrying the empty briefcase. Light rain fell outside, dampening the ground. The woman waited for the crosswalk light. Carter slowed and pretended to look at his phone. The walk sign came on and he followed her across.

She headed down James Street, south towards Pioneer Square at a fast pace. He let the gap between them stretch to half a block. No sense in spooking her. She veered left onto tree-lined Occidental Ave. Carter followed. The road underfoot turned from asphalt to wet brick. Cast-iron lamp posts with white glass globes lit the sidewalks under the trees. This was the old part of town. Where was she headed? He followed her into the park. She stopped under one of the trees. Carter watched from a distance as she made a call on her phone.

A figure crossed the park toward her location. As the person approached, she put away her phone and said something. It was too far away for Carter to hear their conversation. Why was one of Rakman's people meeting strangers in the park at night? She handed over something from her pocket. Drugs? Carter resisted the urge to move closer. The shadowy figure departed. The woman pulled her jacket tight and continued her walk. She exited the far side of the park. Carter followed, wary now that he knew there were others in the area that may know her. It was stupid for him to be doing this. He'd follow her for a few more minutes and then return to the Precinct.

Carter lost sight of her as she turned down an alley. It was hard to see. The only light came from the widely spaced streetlights and their reflections in the wet pavement. Carter stopped at the corner of the building. He had to be careful. He'd once had a mark double-back on him in an alley like this. The experience had left a scar on his chin and a heightened sense of paranoia. Carter glanced around the corner. She was halfway down the narrow lane between the two buildings. It was wide enough to back a garbage truck down to empty the dumpster sitting mid-way between the woman and where he was standing.

Carter crouched low and scurried forward, hugging the wall until he reached the side of the dumpster. It smelled of rotting vegetables and urine. He breathed through his mouth to try and avoid gagging from the stench. A shadowy figure stepped out of an alcove further down the alley. The woman stopped and took a step backward. It was a man. He held up his empty hands. The woman was angry. Carter strained to hear what she was saying.

She jabbed a finger at the person. "—five weeks, Sal. You should have kept in touch."

"I sent texts." Sal didn't sound sorry.

"You know that's not how this works."

"I was busy."

The woman widened her foot placement into a combat stance. "You have a death wish?"

"No."

"Then tell me where you've been."

"I can't."

The woman's hand moved under her jacket. "You can't or you won't?"

"They'll kill me if I tell you."

The woman pulled a knife out of her coat. It looked like the ones from the crime scenes, except the symbols on hers were glowing green. The rain sizzled as it struck the metal surface. "I could kill you now just for missing our last meeting."

Sal took a step back. "I had no choice. I was summoned."

"By who?"

"My Queen."

The woman stepped closer to the man. "Is she responsible for the murders?"

Carter set his briefcase down and drew his gun. He hoped he wouldn't need to use it, but the way the woman was swinging the knife around made him feel less than optimistic.

Sal held up his hands. "There's a war coming, Nadja."

She waved the blade at Sal. "What the hell is that supposed to mean?"

"The Queen knows about the girl."

"What girl?"

Sal shook his head. "The Wardens can't protect her forever."

Nadja pressed the blade against the man's shirt. "Why is your Queen so interested in some girl?"

Carter flipped the safety off on his gun. From his position behind the dumpster he had a protected line of fire. Now, would be a good time to call for backup, but that would mean dealing with the Chief. She wouldn't forgive him for not doing what she'd ordered. *Come on Sal, answer the question so we can all go home.*

Sal smiled cruelly. "I don't know, but she said when they find her—your world will end."

Nadja punched Sal in the face. He barely flinched. Carter had never seen anyone take a blow to the head like that. His skull had to be made of cement. "Don't ever threaten me, Sal."

"I'm just telling you the truth." The man rubbed his jaw. "You should get out of here, Nadja."

She held the knife under Sal's nose. "Is that another threat?"

"No. They're coming though—I don't want you to end up like the others."

Nadja pushed him back against the building with the tip of the blade. "Are you talking about the Wardens that were killed?"

Sal looked away. "I've already said too much."

"You're coming with me. The Council's going to—"

A gust of wind rushed through the narrow space. Something huge dropped from the sky and landed at the far end of the alleyway. The impact shook the ground and made the dumpster lid rattle.

WHAT LIES IN THE ALLEY

Carter's breath caught in his throat. It was huge—larger than an elephant and covered with black scales. It filled the entire alley beyond Nadja and Sal. Was it an animal? A hissing sound filled the air. Billowing clouds of steam rose off the thing. It stood on hind legs and stalked forward, changing size and shape as it approached. Seconds later, it looked like a seven-foot-tall humanoid—except for the pie-shaped reptilian head at the end of its too long neck.

The thing spoke in a raspy voice to Nadja. "He's not going anywhere with you, Warden."

Carter swallowed. After twenty-five years of investigations—this was now the weirdest case.

Nadja's knife glowed bright green, casting an eerie light that threw wild shadows onto the dirty brick walls. A gun appeared in her other hand. The weapon wasn't like any firearm that Carter had ever seen. She aimed it at Sal and pointed the knife at the approaching creature. "You've signed your death warrant showing up like that."

The creature hissed at her. It was laughing. "I don't follow your Laws anymore, Warden." It stalked closer.

Carter raised his gun. Whatever this thing was, he couldn't allow it to hurt the woman. He edged out into the alley trying to get a line of fire that would avoid hitting her.

Sal raised his hands. "I tried to warn you, Nadja."

She glared at him. "Don't move a muscle, Sal."

The creature was within reach of Nadja. Carter cursed under his breath. He stood with his gun leveled at the thing. "Everyone freeze! Seattle Police Department." His voice echoed in the tight space.

The creature's head swiveled up and locked eyes with him.

Nadja glanced at Carter. "You shouldn't have—"

Sal snarled and lunged at her. The sound was like something that should have come from a lion. The skin on Sal's face peeled away like wet tissue paper as his head and body swelled. His clothes ripped revealing glossy black scales.

Nadja jumped back and fired her gun. The weapon made an odd whine-cough noise as green light flashed from the muzzle. The thing that had been Sal recoiled from the shots.

Nadja darted forward and sank her knife deep into use-to-be-Sal's chest. The blade flared bright green. A wave of emerald fire swept outward from the wound consuming Sal's scaly flesh. What was left crumbled into a smoldering pile of ash.

Carter didn't have time to process what he'd seen. The other creature roared and knocked Nadja into the wall of the alley. She bounced off the brick and collapsed on the pavement. Then it charged at him.

What the hell was it!? Carter emptied his magazine into the thing. It shrugged the bullets off like bee-stings and kept coming. He stumbled backward. It closed the distance and grabbed him. Searing pain lanced through his shoulder as its clawed hand tore through his jacket and punctured the skin around his collarbone. It lifted him off the ground. The pain was nauseating. It pulled him upward until his face was level with its hideous head. Its hot breath smelled of rotten meat as it whispered. "Your time has passed. We will soon rule this world."

Carter gritted his teeth. His shoulder screamed in pain. He squinted at the thing's monstrous face. "Damn, you're ugly." It was a dumb thing to say, but the pain was making it hard to think straight.

Nadja's voice came from behind the creature. "—and stupid."

The monster's body thrashed sending ripples of pain through Carter's shoulder. A wave of green fire swept over its scales leaving charred flesh in its wake. The creature's arm disintegrated. Carter dropped to the pavement. Ash and embers fell around him as the thing's body collapsed into dust. He pushed his palm against the bleeding puncture wounds in his shoulder. His vision blurred. He was losing a lot of blood.

Nadja stood over him. Smoke rose off the blade clutched in her hand. The green light was fading from the symbols etched into the side of the metal. "You almost got yourself killed again, Detective."

Carter blinked away tears of pain as he looked up at Nadja. "What was—"

He passed out before he could finish his thought.

4

DEJA VU

"Detective Malloy." The speaker sounded far away. Carter was sitting on something soft. Leather. His shoulder ached.

"Detective Malloy." The voice was closer now. He recognized it. Rakman. Carter opened his eyes. He was back in Leopold Rakman's office. Sitting in one of the fancy leather chairs. The old man leaned against the edge of the desk. "So good to see you awake, Detective."

Carter pushed himself up in the chair and rubbed his face. "How did I get here?" Drops of rain left streaks in the massive window that formed the far wall. It was dark outside. The city lights refracted in the raindrops.

"One of my associates brought you after your unfortunate encounter."

Encounter. The events came flooding back. Carter gripped the arms of the chair. "What the hell was that thing?"

Rakman drummed his fingers on the desk. "Can I interest you in some tea?"

"No. I want to know what just happened!" Carter tried to

stand, but the strength seemed to have left his legs. He slumped back in the chair.

"Are you sure? It will help with the pain and weakness. We had to give you a mild sedative while we healed your wounds."

Carter's shoulder throbbed. He ground his teeth. "Fine."

Rakman waved at someone outside his field of view. The receptionist appeared carrying a silver serving tray with cups and a teapot. She set it down on the desk and left. Rakman poured tea into one of the cups. "Cream and sugar?"

"No."

"I thought not, but people's tastes often change." The old man handed him the cup. It wasn't as hot as Carter had expected. He gulped it down. "Are you going to tell me what happened—what that thing was?"

Rakman laughed. "You've said those same words every time."

"What the hell is that supposed to mean?"

"Detective, would you believe me if I told you we'd met before?"

"Maybe. I've met a lot of people. My memory isn't what it used to be."

Rakman nodded. "If we keep doing this, your memory is going to get worse. This is the fifth time we've sat across from each other in this office."

What was he talking about? Fifth time? Carter had never been here before today. He would have remembered.

"I can tell you don't believe me. That's alright—you never believe me. Let me put your mind at ease, Detective. This place—my people—we protect this world from things like what you saw tonight."

Carter's vision was getting fuzzy. "She killed them with one of those knives. They turned to ash."

"Indeed. The blades are very effective. Those things, as you call them, usually follow our Laws. Something has changed."

"A war. They said something about a war—and a girl." Carter felt himself sliding sideways in the chair.

Rakman's lips pressed together. "Don't worry Detective. They won't get to Miss Ward. Even if they do, they may regret it."

"Who?" Carter had trouble forming the word.

The old man stood. "There's a reason you never remember our conversations, Detective Malloy."

Carter squinted trying to keep him in focus.

Rakman crouched down and whispered in his ear. "It's because you always drink the tea."

Detective Carter Malloy awoke to someone shaking his shoulder.

"Excuse me, sir. You can't sleep here."

It was a police officer. Someone he should probably recognize. Carter stood on unsteady legs. He'd been lying on a bench at a bus stop. He squinted at the officer. "Where am I?"

"Outside the Public Library. Are you okay?"

Carter nodded. His body ached all over. "I'm fine."

"Do you need help getting home?"

"No, I'm fine." The officer nodded and continued his patrol. Carter fished his phone out of his coat. It was Friday night. Friday. The last thing he could remember was going to bed on Sunday. His heart beat faster. It had happened again. He'd lost days. Carter flipped through the calendar and notes on his phone. There were no entries since last week. If there had been anything in there, someone had erased the data.

He started walking back towards the Precinct. Rain spattered the sidewalk. Should he tell the Chief this time? He was only a handful of years from retiring. The only thing he was good at was being a detective. Carter scratched his chin. No. He'd do what he'd done the other times. Ask questions. Try and piece together the missing days. Years of instincts screamed at him. These blackouts weren't some health issue. Someone had done this to him. More than once now. This time he'd be more careful. This time he'd uncover the truth.

Carter smiled to himself. He was a good cop. A better detective. Whoever was responsible was going to regret crossing paths with him. Not today. But someday soon.

AUTHOR'S NOTE

Thank you for taking a chance on a new author—for coming on an adventure with me. Without you, there would be no story—just text on a page. It's your imagination, your emotions, your experiences that breath unique life into these words.

If you enjoyed reading the *The Alley of Secrets*, I would be grateful if you could take a few moments to leave a brief review on the book's Amazon page. Reviews help increase the visibility of my books on the store so that other people like yourself can discover and enjoy them!

To leave a review, visit: **wesleygrandmont.com/books** and click on the Amazon link for *The Alley of Secrets.*

While you're visiting my site, if you're not already a member of my Reader Group, you can join by clicking the button on the main page. I'll send you my monthly newsletter which includes behind-the-scenes information on new and upcoming releases, as well as lots of other great surprises!

Thank you so much for being one of my readers!

-Wes Grandmont III

FREE PREVIEW!

Turn the page to continue the story in the first chapter of
The Obsidian Ascent : Emerald City Dragons - Book 1!

THE HUNT BEGINS

ALLEY

It had been a year since Alley Ward had last killed someone.

She chewed her thumbnail and stole another glance out the plate-glass window of the cafe. The man across the street had been watching her for two days. Did he know she'd been responsible for the accidents? Nothing linked her to the events except the fact that she survived them all.

He was tall with wavy black hair and wore a dark leather jacket with a fleece collar. There was a relaxed intensity to his body. It reminded her of the way a cat acted when it was pretending not to watch its prey.

He looked up at her from his phone. Alley's heart raced. She tried to find something to focus on inside the shop.

Her coworker, Brent, tilted his head towards the windows as he wiped steamed milk off the spout of the espresso machine. "Should I call the cops?"

Alley stared at the cash register. What had she been doing before her mind wandered? "Not yet."

"He's bothering you."

"I'm fine."

Brent fit a plastic lid on a drink and handed it to a customer at the end of the counter. He shuffled over to Alley. Spatters of milk and coffee stained his green apron. He crossed his thick tattooed arms and stared out the window. "I can get rid of him."

Alley rolled her eyes but offered him a smile. "When I need a bodyguard, I'll call you."

A headache clawed at the sides of her skull. The coffee on the bus ride into work wasn't enough anymore. She pressed her hands on the cold counter to steady herself. The flesh toned polish that hid her nails had chipped off in a few places. Most people wouldn't notice the odd maze-like pattern that darkened them or would assume it was decoration—if only that were true.

The morning rush of customers had thinned out. The coffee shop was now full of people on laptops sipping at their drinks. Some were drawn together around tiny circular tables. Soft jazz filled the gaps in their murmurs. Alley knew many of them. The regulars. Working in the cafe was like having her finger on the pulse of the city. It made her feel connected. More than anything, it made her feel normal.

Brent started cleaning one of the blenders. "How's your biology paper going?"

"Good. Research is done, and I've got the first draft. Still needs work though." Alley grabbed a bag of coffee beans and pulled at the top of the sealed package.

"Cool. Cool. So, there's a party this weekend at Jack's place. You want to go? My band will be playing."

Alley had gone to one of their practice sessions a month ago. Brent played guitar and sang backup vocals. He was good. Really good. The kind of good that made you wonder why he was working four days a week at a coffee shop. The rest of the band was okay, but Brent's guitar playing was magic.

She pulled harder on the bag of coffee. It was refusing to open. Then it ripped. Beans spilled across the counter and out onto the floor. Heat rushed to her face as people in the cafe looked up from their screens.

Brent dried his hands and retrieved a broom and dustpan. "Let me help you."

"Thanks."

Alley dragged a waste basket over to the mess and swept beans off the counter into the trash. "I'd love to hear you play again, but I can't—"

Brent bobbed his head as he swept. "—Yeah. No problem. I figured."

Alley touched his arm. "It's my dad. You know—"

"Yeah, no, it's cool. Family first. I respect that." He ran his fingers through his sandy hair and carried the dustpan to the garbage.

Alley reached for another bag of coffee and pulled at the top. This one opened without incident. She poured it into the espresso machine's hopper.

This was the fifth time that Brent had asked her to one of his band's gigs. It was obvious he was interested in being more than friends. There wasn't anything wrong with that. She liked talking to him—liked working with him, but her life was complicated in ways that made relationships difficult. Her schedule was packed between her job, classes and caring for her father. But it was the other stuff that made it really hard. The things she couldn't open up about.

Brent put away the broom and rejoined her by the counter. "So, if a party is out of the question, how about a cup of coffee?"

Her head was still throbbing. Coffee was probably a good idea. "Sure."

He reached for two paper cups and shook them with a grin. "What'll it be?"

"Espresso." It got rid of the headaches faster than drip coffee.

"Coming right up!" He pulled shots of espresso into the cups and gave one to her.

Alley's hand was shaking as she took the drink. A stab of pain lanced through her head. Her cup dropped to the floor. She squeezed her eyes shut and pressed her thumbs into her temples. She hadn't had an episode in over a year. Not since the last accident. She squinted at the digital clock above the carafes. Three hours. It normally took at least seven before the effects of her morning coffee started to wear off.

Alley felt Brent's hand on her elbow. "Are you okay?"

She didn't know whether to nod or shake her head. Usually, she could regain control, but it could get worse. Much worse.

"Can I get you something?"

Alley gritted her teeth. "Coffee. I need more coffee."

Squinting, she glimpsed wispy, golden ribbons of power leaking from her head. They poured out of her in surges that coincided with the stabs of pain. The energy was invisible to everyone else, but that didn't make it less deadly. The snack displays on the counter rattled. A stack of cups beside the register toppled to the ground. The beans in the hopper danced and skittered like kernels of corn popping. Alley pushed on her temples harder. An image exploded in her mind.

She was standing on the peak of a wind-swept mountain covered in snow at the edge of a dark precipice. It was night, but moonlight made the snow sparkle. Orange embers drifted up from the blackness carrying the smell of sulfur. A voice echoed from below. "Join me, child."

"Alley, drink this!" Brent's voice pulled her back.

She grabbed the offered cup and gulped it down. The bitter liquid burned her throat. It hit her stomach. The pain melted away and the rattling in the cafe subsided.

Alley rubbed at her face. Only Brent seemed to have noticed the episode. Espresso was spreading into a wide puddle around the fallen cups at her feet.

Brent's face was lined with worry. "Are you okay?"

"Yeah, I'm fine now. Thanks."

"Does that happen a lot?"

If only he knew. "It's nothing."

Brent looked down at the cups. "Right. Look, whatever it is, you can trust me."

"There's nothing to say. I get migraines sometimes. Coffee helps. End of story." But the hallucination was new. And it had been so vivid.

Brent lowered his voice. "Migraines don't make things fall off counters."

"It was probably just a tremor." He didn't look convinced. She swallowed.

Brent bent over and tossed cups into the recycle bin. "Look, if you want to head out early today, I'll cover for you."

Alley grabbed some paper towels and crouched down beside him. Maybe it was a lack of sleep—the research paper had been keeping her up late. "Thanks. It probably wouldn't hurt for me to lie down." Why did he have to be so nice? It would be easier if he were a jerk. Someone she could push out of her life without feeling guilty. But he wasn't. She hated and appreciated him for it.

She pressed the towels into the brown puddle. "You know on second thought, if I can wrap things up with my dad early on Saturday, maybe I can meet you at Jack's."

Brent smiled. He stood and tossed the last of the cups into the bin. "I'll make sure you have the best night of your life!"

She smiled back. "I'll hold you to that."

"I'm serious about covering for you. Get out of here and get some rest."

She looked around the cafe one last time, then glanced out the front windows.

Her stalker was gone.

Alley felt someone watching as she pushed through the front doors of the coffee shop and out into the cold air. The Seattle morning commuters usually thinned out by noon, but Westlake Plaza was still bustling with tourists fresh off the monorail. She looked over her shoulder expecting to see the stalker following, but the street was just a blur of unfamiliar faces. She hitched her backpack higher onto her shoulder and walked faster down the street. Her phone said it was almost 10:00. If she hurried, she might catch the next bus.

The stop was a block and a half away. As she moved further from the plaza, the crowded sidewalk thinned out. Her auburn ponytail bounced in time with the pace of her footsteps. A chill October wind blew up the street, blasting her in the face.

Someone's gaze was burning a hole in her spine. Half an empty block back, a man in a red hooded sweatshirt was following her. It wasn't the guy who had been watching her the past few days. This was someone new.

He met her gaze.

Alley swallowed. There was something unnatural about his eyes.

She ran.

Up ahead, a line was forming for the bus.

The sidewalk pounded against her feet. She glanced back. The man in the sweatshirt was in pursuit.

Alley faced forward just in time to glimpse a person stepping into her path as she slammed into them. An old man in a tweed trench-coat.

He caught her arm, saving her from falling. "Is everything okay, Miss Ward?"

Alley's lungs burned. The stalker in the red sweatshirt was going to catch up. She turned, but couldn't see him. She scanned up and down the street. He had vanished.

"Miss Ward?"

She faced the old man. He peered at her over the wire rims of spectacles perched on the end of a pointed nose. He was thin with short white hair and piercing gray eyes.

Alley struggled to catch her breath. "Sorry—who are you?"

He smiled as he reached into his coat and withdrew a business card. "My name is Leopold Rakman. I'm a colleague of your father, Benjamin Ward."

Alley took the card. It was black with *Rakman & Associates* printed in silver lettering. The office address was in the Columbia Center. Alley looked up. "I'll tell him we met."

The bus arrived at the stop. There was still no sign of the man in the red sweatshirt.

"Please do. And if it's not too much trouble, will you

deliver a message for me? Tell him, the Council can't wait any longer. We're taking matters into our own hands. He'll understand what that means."

"Okay." Cryptic, but whatever. The vehicle doors opened. "I'm sorry—I have to catch this bus." She pocketed the card and glanced up and down the street again. Passengers boarded.

Rakman pushed his spectacles up the bridge of his narrow nose. "It was a pleasure bumping into you, Miss Ward. I look forward to our paths crossing again."

She smiled and nodded. "Yeah, sorry about that. I'll deliver the message."

He waved with a gloved hand as she ran towards the bus. The doors started to shut. Alley jammed her foot into the narrowing gap.

The driver frowned as the doors hissed back open. "Next time, get here earlier."

Alley nodded as the doors clamped shut behind her. She grabbed at the metal railing overhead and made her way to an empty seat in the back as the bus pulled away. Out the window, the old man receded into the distance. Something about his presence had spooked the stalker. She swung her pack off her shoulder, sank into one of the blue seats and wiped moisture off her brow with a sleeve.

Alley pulled out the black business card. *Leopold Rakman.* She felt bad about almost knocking him down. She'd never met anyone that worked with her father. Dad was secretive about the classified projects in his lab. A few times each month, a shuttle would arrive to take him there for the day. She could remember going there as a small child, but hadn't been there in a long time. He said it was for her safety—that she'd already been effected enough by the place.

The bus was mostly empty. Alley unzipped her pack and put on her earbuds. A song with a mix of classical violin and electric baseline streamed out of her phone. She leaned her head back against the seat and closed her eyes. Her mind drifted.

Cold. Nighttime. Moonlight glinting off fresh snow. Glowing embers. She was standing at the edge of the dark precipice again. Heat and the smell of sulfur wafted upward as a gust of wind blew her hair away from her face.

The silky female voice she'd heard before came from the dark. "Join me, child."

Alley squinted, trying to see what lay in the blackness. Two glowing lavender orbs appeared. They blinked. Eyes. Enormous eyes. Alley swallowed and tried to step back. Her feet were encased in ice.

"There is nowhere you can hide from me."

A high-pitched chime sounded in her ear. Someone had sent her a text message. Alley's heart raced. Her forehead felt damp. She could still feel the cold grip of ice around her ankles. The bus was on the 520-bridge crossing Lake Washington. Back to the Eastside. To Redmond. To home. She took a deep breath and slowly let it out. The sky was clear. Across the lake, Mt. Rainier's massive peak rose to the south. Every time she saw it, the mountain seemed bigger than she remembered. She rubbed her eyes and tapped the message on the phone.

It was from Elek. *"Hey Al. Back in town. Want to hang?"*

Alley couldn't help but smile. She typed a reply and hit send. *"Been a while. Where you been?"*

A moment later Elek replied. *"Long story. You know me."*

Alley smirked and tapped a response. *"Thought you found a new best friend."*

"Tried. Failed. Guess you'll have to do."

She stifled a laugh as she typed. "*Your failure pleases me.*"

A new message appeared. "*LOL. So you interested in catching up?*"

She did, but she needed to rest. She sighed as she responded. "*Been a rough day. U going to be around long?*"

His answer came a few seconds later. "*A bit.*"

"*Got time tomorrow night?*"

He answered. "*Yeah, I should be around.*"

She smiled. "*See you then.*"

Alley clicked on her photo album and scrolled back through a year's worth of pictures. She tapped the first one she saw of Elek. She'd taken it the day they had graduated from high school. His green gown and cap were in a pile on the stone wall beside him. He was wearing a gray shirt and black jeans. His lanky arms were crossed. His dark eyes peered at the camera through a mop of tousled black hair. He was the closest thing she had to a brother.

What had he been up to for the last year and a half? She swiped through a few more pictures. Shots of them hiking in the Olympics, a bonfire on a wide flat beach roasting marshmallows. Skiing. Covered in scrapes from a wipe-out on a mountain bike. A shot of him swimming after an oar. They'd had some good times growing up, but they'd lost touch over the last year. She'd gotten busy with classes and work. He'd started a night job that meant he was sleeping whenever she was awake. They still sent texts, but it wasn't like the old days. It would be good to see him again.

Alley pushed the power button on the side of the phone and watched the screen darken as the bus pulled into the Redmond Transit Center. She got off and boarded the second bus. Fifteen minutes later, she was walking up the tree-lined street to her house. A nap would be good. Hopefully one free of dreams.

Autumn was turning the trees to shades of flame. As she approached the house, fallen leaves skittered across the cracked concrete of the driveway. Moss grew on the roof of the porch. The white paint on the clapboards was peeling.

And the front door hung open.

———

Alley swallowed. Her tongue was dry. Was her father okay? She ran up the creaky porch steps and entered the house.

Inside was silent except for the ticking of a clock in the living room.

"Dad?"

No answer.

Her pulse quickened. Alley dropped her backpack, shut the front door, and moved down the hallway to the back of the house. The door to his study was closed. She tried turning the handle. It was locked from the inside. She rapped her knuckles on the polished wood. "Dad?"

No answer.

She rattled the knob and pounded on the door with her fist. "Dad! Are you in there?"

Still no answer.

Alley ran into the kitchen, opened the cabinet under the sink and pulled out a rusted red toolbox. The lid squeaked as it flopped backward. Tools clattered against each other as she searched for the crowbar. She lifted the heavy iron rod out of the box and ran back to the study.

The flat head of the bar fit into the edge of the door frame near the locking mechanism. How much force would be needed to break through the lock? Alley's heart pounded.

Suddenly, the knob to the study turned, and the door swung inward. Alley dropped the crowbar.

"You're home early!" Her father was seated in his wheel-chair. His thinning white hair stuck out at odd angles. His blue eyes were bright and peered at her through glasses that enlarged the wrinkles around his eyes. He pulled a pair of headphones off, wrapped them around his neck and ran his finger and thumb along his white handlebar mustache.

Alley bent down and hugged him. Her cheeks felt wet.

He wrapped his arms around her, his voice was quiet. "What's wrong?"

Alley let go and stood, brushing the tears away. She forced a smile onto her face. "You weren't answering. I thought—"

A lump formed in her throat. She looked away blinking.

Her father's warm hand rested on hers. "I'm sorry, Buttercup. I didn't hear you. You usually aren't home so early. Is everything alright?"

"I had a headache. Took the rest of the day off."

The lines deepened between his eyebrows. "Must have been a bad one."

She chewed on her lip. "Yeah—it was one of those. I'm okay now."

He squinted at her, then turned his wheelchair and moved back into the study. She followed. The room was lined floor to ceiling with dark polished wood shelves packed with books. Some were old leather-bound tomes, cracked and falling apart, others were newer volumes on science, math, biology, politics and other subjects. Wedged between the books were odd knickknacks. At the back of the room was a workbench strewn with scientific equipment and electronic parts.

Her dad wheeled himself behind a giant oak desk in the center of the room where more books and papers were piled around a flat computer monitor. "Was anyone hurt?"

She shook her head and tried to block out the mental images from the last time it had gotten out of control. Her father rubbed a hand across his forehead. Alley could feel a lecture coming.

"Have you considered increasing your coffee dose?"

She raised an eyebrow. "Dad."

"I just want you to be happy—happy and safe."

She walked around the desk and hugged him. "You don't need to worry. I can handle this."

He smiled with sad eyes. "Your mother used to tell me that."

Alley glanced at the framed photo of her mom on the desk. They had the same auburn hair. The same amber eyes. Twelve years she'd been gone. The explosion at her parent's research lab had almost claimed both of them. Almost. She stared at her reflection in the polished chrome of her Dad's wheelchair. The accident hadn't just taken her mom and maimed her father. It had destroyed her mother's research notes.

Alley straightened. "I wish Mom had told you more." It was hard to believe that they'd worked in the same lab and her father had so little understanding of her work. Her dad only knew that Alley had accidentally been exposed to something and her mother had been trying to find a way to reverse her condition. At least he'd known enough about her findings to suggest that coffee could dampen the effects.

He looked away. "Me too."

Alley fished the business card out of her pocket. "I met someone you work with—Leopold Rakman?"

Her father reached for the card with a shaky hand.

"He asked me to deliver a message."

Her father's thumb rubbed across the silver foil letters

on the card. When he spoke, his voice was low. "What did he say?"

"Something about the Council taking matters into their own hands?"

"Did he say when?"

"No, that was it. I feel bad. I literally ran into him."

Her father placed the card on the desk. He massaged his hand between his thumb and forefinger.

Alley picked up a small stone statue, engraved with detailed patterns. "Does he know about me?"

Her dad nodded. "He knows enough. You can trust him."

"Then why do you look so concerned?"

"It's probably nothing."

She put down the statue. "Should I be worried?"

"I have to make a few calls. We can talk later."

"You sure?"

He touched her arm. "You should get some rest, Buttercup. I love you."

"I love you too, Dad." What wasn't he telling her? She walked into the hall and bent down to pick up the crowbar. "Holler if you need anything."

He nodded as he picked up his phone.

Alley moved back into the kitchen and put away the tools. The message had rattled him so much that she hadn't had a chance to talk about the stalker. Or the dreams.

A pot of coffee from earlier in the morning was warming on the coffee maker hot plate. She pulled a mug out of the cabinet, filled it with the dark liquid and carried it upstairs to her bedroom.

Afternoon sun poured in through the window spilling across her desk and bed. Alley took a big sip of coffee and set the mug down on the night table. It tasted burned. She sat down on the edge of the bed and kicked off her shoes.

What a crazy day. Her research books were stacked on the desk next to her laptop. Her biology project was almost done, but she couldn't focus on it right now. The morning had been so stressful. It had been a long time since she'd had an episode. It could have been bad.

Her scrapbook rested on the corner of the desk. She picked it up and set it in her lap. The cover said, *"Never Forget..."*

She opened to the first page. A photocopy of an old newspaper clipping lay beneath a thin layer of plastic. The headline read, *"Child lone survivor in highway bridge collapse."* She brushed her finger across the words. *I'm sorry.* Her chest ached.

She turned the page to another newspaper clipping. *"Bus crushed in rock-slide, students survive with minor injuries."* She felt her eyes watering. *I'm so sorry.*

She flipped past a dozen more pages to the clipping on the last page. *"Prom night turns deadly."* She skimmed the familiar report. *"—the bodies of the three students were found in the debris. It's not certain at this time what caused the collapse of the east hallway. Investigators will be examining the rest of the school over the weekend to determine if it is safe for students to return to classes next week—"*

A tear splashed on the plastic page of the scrapbook. Alley wiped at her face, then reached for the coffee mug and took a huge gulp. She couldn't lose control again. She'd start doubling her coffee intake. Whatever it took.

Alley closed the scrapbook and put it back on the desk. Someday she'd find a way to make-up for all the harm she had caused. To help people instead of—she shook her head. One step at a time. She had to complete her pre-med courses, and right now that meant finishing her research paper. But first, her chipped nail polish needed fixing. It kept people from asking questions she didn't know the answers to.

Alley opened the drawer to her nightstand, pulled out a bottle of pink polish and shook it. She twisted the cap off, brushed a coat onto each of her fingers and blew on them gently until they were dry. Better. Alley closed the bottle and pulled her hair out of its ponytail. She flopped back onto her pillow. Nap time. Brent was a lifesaver. She owed him one.

Her eyes slid shut.

Cold wind clawed at her hair and clothes. Alley clutched her arms tight across her body. The snow was up to her knees. The moon shined high overhead, painting the mountainside in silvery light. Ahead a ridge rose, black against the night sky. Hundreds of dark forms moved towards her down the slopes.

Alley felt her stomach twist into a knot. She turned and started running. Air from her lungs formed cold clouds of vapor as she high stepped through the thick snow. She glanced back over her shoulder. Some of the things had reached the base of the mountain and were bounding through the drifts. She couldn't see what they were, just a mass of darkness thrashing against the shimmering white.

Ahead of her, the snow thinned and gave way to jagged rocks and gravel ending at a small peak. She ran up the slope. Her thighs and lungs were burning. Loose stones slipped beneath her feet. Alley stumbled forward, pushing herself upward. She turned as she reached the summit. The small peak was surrounded by snowy slopes. From every direction came a swarming mass of scaly black bodies.

She was trapped.

A deep female voice echoed across the valley. "I am coming for you."

The creatures crawled over one another in their haste. Alley clenched her hands into fists. They reached the bottom of the slope and made their way upwards. All she could see were their eyes, hundreds of eyes the color of jewels. And then their claws. Teeth. Dark Scales. Her heart thundered inside her chest.

The monsters leaped towards her.

Beep! Beep! Beep!

The sound of her bedside alarm clock brought her back. Alley turned it off and rubbed at her face. She squinted at the digital display. Four in the morning. An hour to catch the bus to work. Ugh. She hadn't planned on sleeping that long. She swung her legs onto the floor. Her body proceeded on auto-pilot going through her morning routine of showering, dressing and wandering downstairs.

The smell of freshly brewed coffee filled the kitchen. Dad was awake and had pulled his wheelchair up to the round breakfast table.

"Good morning, Buttercup!"

"Mmmm." She nodded at him as she shuffled towards the coffee pot. She grabbed a mug and filled it.

"You slept right through dinner. I thought you'd be starving." He gestured towards the stove. "I made pancakes and eggs. Your favorite!"

She set her mug down, pulled on an oven mitt and opened the door to the stove. Inside a plate of pancakes and scrambled eggs was warming. "Thanks, Dad." She brought it over to the table, then returned to the counter to retrieve her coffee and a fork. She came back and sat down across from him.

"I made some calls while you were sleeping. We need to talk this evening. There's some people I need to introduce to you."

Alley nodded her head as she chewed on a mouthful of eggs, then stopped. She'd told Elek she'd have time to catch up with him tonight. She swallowed. "Elek is back in town. I said I'd be around this evening."

Her father frowned. "It's not something I can put off any longer. Elek will understand."

Alley took a big gulp of coffee. "Okay. I'll let him know I'll be late." She cut into the stack of pancakes with the side of her fork and pushed a chunk into her mouth.

Her dad shifted in his seat and adjusted his glasses. "Is everything okay? You slept a long time."

Alley took a sip of coffee and checked the wall clock in the kitchen. Fifteen minutes to catch the bus. "I had a strange dream."

Her father steepled his fingers. "Would you tell me about it?"

"Standard nightmare stuff. I was being chased by monsters."

Her father leaned in. "What else do you remember?"

Alley pushed the eggs around on her plate. "It was snowing, and there was a voice."

"What did it say?"

"That it was coming for me."

He started massaging his hand. "You should call in sick."

"I feel fine." Why was he stressing about a dream?

"Please. It would give us a chance to talk."

Alley got up from the table. "I'd love to Dad, but Brent covered for me yesterday. We'll talk tonight. I promise."

He sighed. "Be careful."

Alley gave him a hug. "I'm careful every day." He still looked stressed, but she was going to miss the bus. She poured the rest of her coffee into a travel mug, grabbed her backpack and headed down the hallway towards the front door.

"I love you, Buttercup." He blew her a kiss.

She caught it and blew one back. "I love you too."

Alley stepped off the bus onto 5th and Pine. The gray sky was brightening as the morning sun tried to burn through the clouds. Commuters bundled in fall jackets and scarves rushed to work. Everyone seemed to be going somewhere, and there was no sign of her stalker. Dry leaves crunched under her sneakers as she walked along the red, black and gray bricks of the plaza. The plate-glass walls of the single-story coffee shop sat ahead on the corner of the block. She walked faster, reached the front doors of the building and yanked them open. Heat and the aroma of fresh coffee washed over her.

There were a few people inside ordering. Brent waved at her from behind the counter. He smiled as she came around to join him.

"Morning, Alley!"

How was he always so cheerful? She forced a smile on her face and glanced out the windows of the store. No stalker. She entered the prep room, dropped her bag and jacket in a locker, pulled a green apron over her head and tied it behind her back. Maybe everything would be back to normal today.

"Tall medium roast for Gwen." Brent handed Alley a paper coffee cup. "So, you feeling better today?"

"Yeah, a bit. Thanks for yesterday."

"Oh yeah, it was no problem." He lowered his voice. "I'm here if you ever want to talk about—you know—*stuff*."

She'd hoped Brent wouldn't mention the episode. "Thanks." Her voice came out flat.

Brent's face flushed. He seemed to sense that he had crossed a line. "So anyway—tomorrow night is going to be awesome!"

"I'm looking forward to it too." Alley glanced out the window.

Brent followed her gaze. "He's a no-show today."

Alley nodded, then turned to him. "Can I ask you a favor?"

"Anything."

"Would you mind walking me to the bus stop at the end of my shift?"

Brent's eyebrows raised. "Of course." He crossed his arms and squinted at her. "Is everything okay?"

She swallowed. "There was this guy in a red sweatshirt yesterday. He chased me down 4th street. Freaked me out."

Alley could see the muscles in Brent's forearm flex. His eyes swept across the store and out through the walls of plate-glass. "Thanks for telling me. I'll make sure no one bothers you."

A group of people came in through one of the sets of doors. Alley smoothed her apron. She felt a little relief knowing that Brent would be watching her back. "I'll take orders for a bit."

Brent nodded. "Cool."

Alley smiled as she took the first guests' order. She handed cups to Brent and heated up baked goods. The line grew as more people entered the cafe. She stole glances out the windows. No one was watching her, but her head was starting to ache. She should have more coffee. No more episodes. When they got to the end of this group, she'd pour herself a cup. She counted the people in line. Some faces were familiar, people she knew by name. Others were first-timers. The last person—Alley's heart skipped a beat. It was him—the guy that had been watching her the last few days. He was wearing the same dark leather jacket.

He smiled.

She realized her mouth was hanging open and clamped it shut. What was he doing in here?

She looked at the next person in line. "What can I get for you?"

Alley half listened to the reply, jotting the order on the side of a cup. Should she ask him why he'd been staring at her? Was he dangerous?

She took the orders of the next few people in front of him. Sweat trickled down her spine. He moved up to the counter. He smelled like cedar and rosemary.

Her hands were shaking. She clasped them together. "What can I—"

Before she could finish, he placed a folded piece of brown paper on the counter, turned and walked out of the cafe. Written in the center of the scrap in black flowing ink were six words:

You are in danger. Leave now.

She read it again. Her heart was beating. Should she call the police?

"Alley, everything okay?" Brent was at her side. "Was that who I think it was?"

"Yeah, he gave me this." She handed him the paper.

What kind of danger was she in? She looked around the

shop. There were the regulars and a few new faces. No one looked dangerous. A movement in the back corner caught her eye. A guy sitting at one of the small tables. Bald, with pale skin and a dark goatee. He was watching her.

Brent saw where she was looking. "You think we need to worry about him?"

"I'm not sure—maybe."

The next person in line moved forward, blocking her view.

"Could I please have a tall, dark-roast." It was a short elderly woman with bifocals. Her white hair was tied up in a bun, and she wore a blue shawl around her shoulders.

Alley picked up a cup. "Room for cream?"

The elderly woman shook her head. It swiveled oddly, moving too fast and then slowing too quickly.

Alley blinked and rubbed at the bridge of her nose. "Sorry, was that a no?"

"That's right dear."

Alley punched in the order. "That's a dollar fifty."

The woman reached into her purse and placed two bills on the counter. Her fingernails were long, black and splintered. Alley tried not to stare. The words on the crumpled paper screamed in her head.

You are in danger. Leave now.

Stay calm. Just pick up the cash and give the lady her change.

Brent set the coffee on the counter.

As Alley reached to take the bills, the old woman's hand shot out and grabbed her wrist. It was like a vice. Tight, painful. She tried to pull her arm back, but the woman was too strong. Her head started to throb. *Not now!* She'd had coffee this morning. It was too soon for the effects to have worn off.

Alley gritted her teeth. "Let go!"

You must come with me. The sound of the woman's voice echoed in her head, but her lips weren't moving.

Brent grabbed the woman's arm. "Take your hand off her."

A growl rumbled in the old woman's throat. It made a spike of adrenaline surged through Alley's veins. The sound wasn't human. It was like a lion—or something worse. The old woman reached across the counter with her other hand and shoved Brent. He flew as if he'd been hit by a car, slammed into the back wall and collapsed to the floor.

The shop erupted into chaos. People yelled and ran towards the glass doors.

Brent!

He wasn't moving. Alley had to help him.

There was a metal stand holding a display of mints and candies beside the register. Alley grabbed it with her free hand and smashed it against the old woman's arm. The lady's face contorted into a snarl. Her lips peeled back to reveal sharp black teeth. Alley's heart raced. The woman yanked the stand from Alley's hand and flung it across the shop.

Alley felt her feet leave the floor as she was dragged across the counter. Her body knocked over the coffee cup. The hot liquid soaked into her shirt, burning the skin on her stomach.

A wave of dizziness washed over her. The room went out of focus. Energy leaked from her mind like a dam giving way to flood waters. Everything in the store began to rattle. Metal spoons beat a staccato rhythm against ceramic cups and saucers. Bags of coffee tumbled from shelves. The vibrations intensified as invisible tendrils of energy poured from her mind. A picture dislodged from the wall of the shop and smashed to the ground. Shards of glass skittered across the floor. The store windows fractured and cascaded onto the sidewalk. People in the street were shouting and screaming. Metal crunched as cars collided outside.

Alley's knee hit the floor as she was pulled off the counter. A stab of pain shot up her leg. The old woman was dragging her towards the shattered doors.

Golden ribbons of energy whipped and snapped outward. They tore at the steel beams overhead. Alley could feel the metal bending and tearing. Cracks formed in the ceiling, raining dust and plaster down.

Time seemed to slow as a support girder broke free from the ceiling and swung downward. It crashed into the old woman. She let out a roar as she was knocked down and pinned beneath its weight. The skin on the woman's face peeled away revealing black scales. Alley recognized it—one of the monsters from her dream. It let go of Alley as it tried to push the enormous steel girder off its body. The beam didn't move. The creature howled in frustration. Its black teeth snapped at the air like an angry dog.

Alley scrambled away from the beast. Dust choked the air. The high-pitched hiss of escaping gas was coming from a nearby broken ceiling pipe. The sweet tang of it filled her nostrils.

She had to get Brent out of here.

Alley staggered around the counter. Brent lay where he had fallen. Blood flowed from his ears and nose. He was covered in a layer of debris. She knelt and touched his cheek. *Cold.*

No.

She pressed her finger to the inside of his hand.

Please don't be dead.

Seconds that felt like minutes slipped by. Nothing. Alley shifted her fingers and pressed again.

There was a weak pulse.

A tremor rocked the shop as more energy flowed from her body. A section of the ceiling on the other side of the counter collapsed sending a plume of dust toward them. Alley coughed as it filled her lungs. When the air cleared, a bundle of torn electrical wiring hung from the new hole in the ceiling.

She grabbed Brent under the armpits and tried to drag him. The muscles in her thighs and back burned as she strained to pull him across the floor. The smell of gas was getting stronger. The frayed ends of the exposed electrical wiring swayed back and forth in slow motion. She pulled harder. They had to get out. Another tendril of energy flowed out of Alley. It traveled into the ground, rocking the building. The torn wires swung wildly and brushed by one another. A tiny blue spark jumped between them.

No.

The inside of the shop exploded in a white-hot fireball.

Alley squeezed her eyes shut as a wave of searing heat blasted her skin. Every pore of her body screamed in pain. The oxygen was ripped from her lungs.

Darkness engulfed her mind.

ALSO BY WES GRANDMONT III

Make sure to check out the rest of the books in the *Emerald City Dragons* series!

The Obsidian Ascent : Emerald City Dragons - Book 1

For a complete list, please visit:

wesleygrandmont.com/books

ABOUT THE AUTHOR

Wesley Grandmont III is a writer, artist and game developer who is passionate about crafting immersive worlds for his readers. He writes stories that mix the modern world with magic—urban fantasies with the tension and pacing of espionage thrillers. His debut book series *Emerald City Dragons*, is an urban fantasy world set in and around Seattle.

A seasoned veteran of the video game industry, Wes has worked on over twenty games, most recently as Lead Technical Art Director on Microsoft's *Halo 5 : Guardians*, and Sony's *Ghost of Tsushima*.

When not crafting new stories or games, he loves coffee (lots of coffee), skiing, hiking and spending time with family and friends in the Pacific Northwest.

facebook.com/WesGrandmontAuthor

amazon.com/author/wesgrandmont